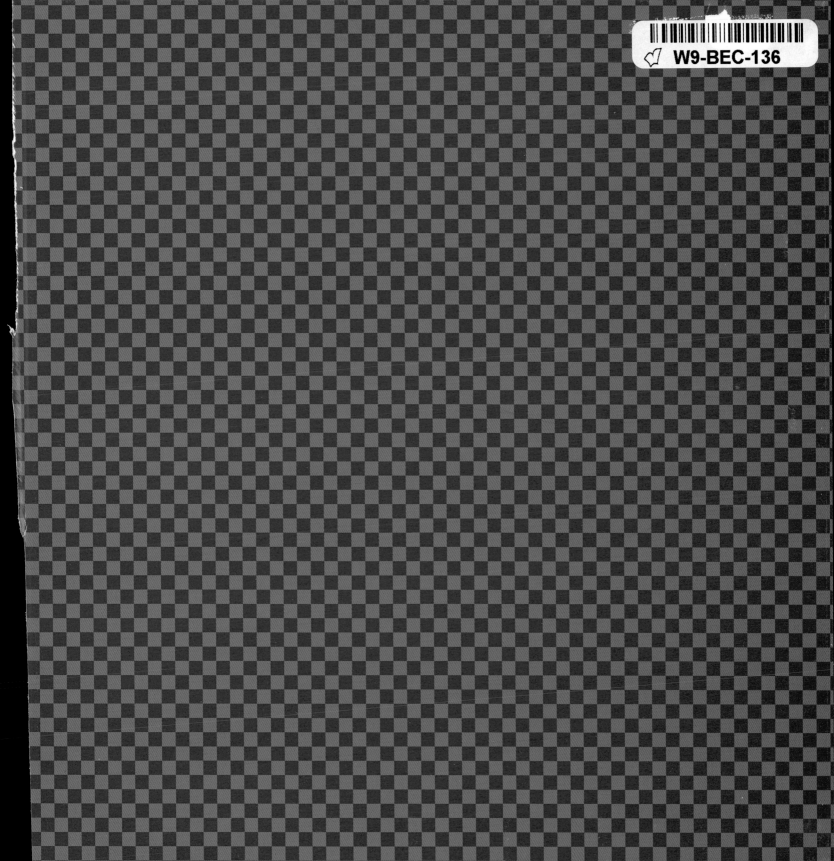

Helping Kids Heal

With My Mom, With My Dad

Written by Maribeth Boelts

Illustrated by Cheri Bladholm

Zonderkidz

Zonder**kidz**®

The children's group of Zondervan

www.zonderkidz.com

With My Mom, With My Dad
Copyright © 2004 by The Zondervan Corporation
Illustrations copyright © 2004 by Cheri Bladholm

Requests for information should be addressed to:
Zonderkidz, *Grand Rapids, Michigan 49530*

Library of Congress Cataloging-in-Publication Data

Boelts, Maribeth, 1964–
  With my mom, with my dad : a book about divorce / by Maribeth Boelts ; [illustrated by Cheri
Bladholm].
     p. cm.
  Summary: On a visit to his father's house and back home with his mother, Justin asks about his parents' divorce and how it affects him, but finds his jumbled emotions calmed when he remembers that he still has the love of both parents and God. Includes a note for parents.
  ISBN 0-310-70644-0 (Hardcover)
  [1. Divorce — Fiction. 2. Parent and child — Fiction. 3. African Americans — Fiction. 4. Christian life — Fiction.] I. Bladholm, Cheri, ill. II. Title.
  PZ7.B635744Wi 2004
  [E] – dc22

                                                                          2003022066

Editor: Gwen Ellis
Art Direction & Design: Laura M. Maitner

Printed in China

05 06 07/ HK /4 3 2

To all children
who are with their mom,
or with their dad.
Maribeth Boelts

To Michael, Janice, and Brendan for modeling
for this book with such compassion and to Shawna for
photography. May the whole Egan family be blessed!
Cheri Bladholm

Justin watched from the apartment window waiting for his dad to pick him up. His stomach twisted, and he felt sick. It was hard to get used to the coming and the going part since the divorce. Finally, Justin saw his dad's vehicle turn into the driveway. He ran down the sidewalk to meet him.

Dad gave him a hug. "Let's say good-bye to your mom before we go," he said, walking Justin back up to the door.

Justin listened to his dad and mom talk for a few minutes. He hoped Dad would give Mom a hug, but he didn't. He wished Mom would say, "Let's get married again," but she didn't.

IN THE CAR, Justin showed Dad a new scrape on his elbow. He told Dad how he had taught his cat, Jupiter, to fetch.

"That's pretty amazing for a cat," Dad said. "Hey! Have you heard any new jokes lately?"

Justin remembered one from school. "Why did the cookie go to the doctor?" he asked.

"I don't know—why?"

"Because he was feeling crummy!" said Justin.

Dad laughed and said it was his best joke yet. The rest of the ride back to Dad's apartment, they sang with the radio like they always did. Dad took the long way so they could hear the rest of their favorite song—the song that used to be his mom's favorite, too. *I wish she was here with us,* Justin thought.

BY THE TIME they got to Dad's apartment, Justin's stomach was growling. At his mom's, they made simple things to eat, but Justin and Dad liked to cook. Dad got out the big cookbook, and together they chose spaghetti and meatballs.

"We always make too much," Dad said as they began to cook. "So we'll put some in the freezer for you to take back home on Sunday."

THE NEXT MORNING, Justin and Dad played soccer at the park, got haircuts, and took a basket of clothes to the Laundromat. It was warm and quiet in the Laundromat, with only the steady whir of the washers and dryers. Watching the clothes tumble, Justin asked the question he had asked several times before. "How come you and Mom don't live together anymore?"

Dad took a deep breath and slowly let it out. He put his hand on Justin's knee. "Your mom and I just couldn't get along anymore. We tried for a long time to work it out, but we just couldn't."

The dryer timer buzzed, but Dad ignored it.

"But...what if I had been a better kid? Would you and Mom still be married then?" Justin asked.

"Son, you did nothing wrong," Dad said. "And you are not in any way the cause of our divorce. I want you to believe that."

Justin nodded, but he wasn't sure he believed it at all.

ON SUNDAY, Justin and Dad went to church. Justin liked his dad's church. It was different from the one he and his mom attended. A lady with red tennis shoes waved her hands in the air when she sang. A man in the back row said "Amen" and "Yes" when he liked something the pastor said.

After church, Dad turned the radio on, but neither one of them sang. As the rain came down, drops of water chased each other on the car windshield.

Justin swallowed hard. "When I'm with you, I miss Mom, but when I'm with Mom, I miss you."

"I know," Dad said, as he brushed Justin's hair back with his hand. "It's really hard when we're not together."

MOM HAD a peanut butter and honey sandwich waiting for Justin when he came in the door. She listened while Justin told her all about the spaghetti and meatballs, playing soccer, and the lady at church with the red tennis shoes.

"It's great that you had a good weekend with your dad," Mom said, as Justin gave her a hug.

THAT EVENING, Justin and Mom went Rollerblading and talked for a long time, even about the hard stuff.

"If parents can stop loving each other, can they stop loving their kids?" Justin asked.

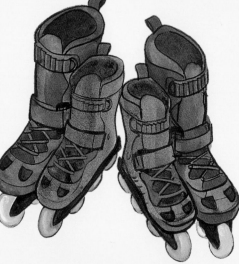

Mom put her arm around Justin's shoulder. "Oh, Justin—even when parents get divorced, they never stop loving their children. Dad and I have loved you from the minute we knew God was creating you—and that love has grown."

Justin leaned into his mom's arms, listening as Mom told him that things were going to get better day by day. "It won't always be as difficult as it is right now," she said.

THAT NIGHT, Justin brushed his teeth. He tried to concentrate on the story his mom read to him. After she had kissed him goodnight, he tossed and turned in his bed. All of a sudden, he felt mad and sad and mixed-up at the same time.

Even though God already knew, Justin told him that he didn't like the way things were since the divorce. He talked to God about all the things he didn't understand until there weren't any words left.

Then he remembered something...

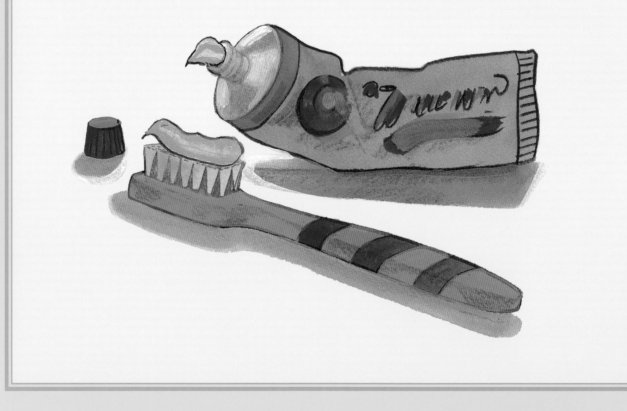

Each night, when Dad tucked him in, he always said, "God loves you, Justin, and so do I."

And each night, when Mom tucked him in, she always said, "God loves you, Justin, and so do I."

Justin listened to Jupiter's low purr, counted the stars that glowed on his ceiling, and thought and thought, until it was very late.

Then he thanked God for his mom and dad, and for God's love that always stays the same, no matter what kind of tough things happen in a kid's life.

And even though Justin fell asleep before he could say, "Amen," he knew that God had heard him.

When a Child Is Facing His Parents' Divorce

When a child's parents divorce, that child frequently will struggle with difficult feelings. It is quite common for children to believe "myths" about divorce. Those myths are:

- I caused the divorce.
- I have to choose which parent to love.
- Some day they will get back together.
- I have to get them back together.

Parents can directly or inadvertently encourage a child to believe these ideas, but when children believe these it creates emotional conflict and pain in them. Parents must deal with the reality of a divorce that has occurred. The reality is that the child did not cause the divorce, that the child must not and cannot choose between parents, that in all likelihood parents will not reunite, and that there is nothing the child can do to make the parents reunite. Parents need to be aware that their child is vulnerable to believing these myths and they need to address the reality of divorce.

Divorce is not pretty. It is painful. Parents hurt too when they divorce. No one marries planning to or preparing to divorce. Parents must put the needs of their children over their own needs or concerns. While this is always true, it is often a much more difficult task after a divorce.

In the book *With My Mom, With My Dad* we find an excellent example of the struggles that children and parents go through during and following a divorce. The answer as to why parents divorce is not easy, but the fault is never the child's. Use this book to underscore certain truths your child needs to understand.

Though no longer husband and wife, you are still Mom and Dad. You still love your child and you always will.

You understand your child's hurt and your child's confusion. It is normal to hurt and it would be strange to not feel hurt and loss in this situation.

Remember that time will help you all adjust, but hurt can still remain.

It's all right to talk about times when Mom and Dad were still married. It is very important for your child to recall that at one time your family was together and at one time Mom and Dad loved each other so much that you had a child together.

Even though God hates divorce because of what it does to his children, he is always there and his love never changes.

Your child has a future that will be good, a future in which your child can be certain of the love and the presence of you and of God.

Talk to your child. Remind your child over and over again of these things. Use this book to encourage you and your child to face these emotions.

When a divorce takes place there is a legal finalization of the divorce. However, it can take a much longer time to recognize the reality and the permanence of the divorce. This "emotional finalization" of a divorce can take place in stages over time. Remember that your child might struggle with emotions and the myths regarding divorce at various times and long after the divorce is complete. Read and re-read this book to help you and your child make a health connection and to encourage your child's connection with God.

A Word to Parents and Other Caregivers

Everyday life in God's world presents challenges and problems for all of us. Children, as well as adults, struggle with a variety of feelings when faced with emotionally charged situations. By helping our children clearly recognize God's loving presence in their lives—that he is with them no matter what happens—we help to prepare them for life. One of the names of Jesus Christ is "Emmanuel, God with us," and God with us is the pervasive theme of this Helping Kids Heal series. The books honestly and sensitively address the difficult emotions children face.

Children love a good story, and stories can provide a safe way to approach issues, concerns, and problems. Therapists who work with children have long used stories to help children acknowledge emotions they would rather avoid. When a loving parent, a kind grandparent, or a caring teacher reads about a story character who is experiencing difficult feelings, the child has permission to feel, to ask questions, to voice his or her fears, and to struggle with emotions. Remember, as with any good story, one reading is never enough. Repetition is a great reminder of the truths contained in the story.

Each child is different. Some children, when facing a difficult emotion, will ask questions and wonder aloud about the characters in the books. Other children are content to just listen and take it all in. After several readings, try to draw them out to talk about the story. You, more than anyone else, will know what the child needs. Keep these things in mind as you use these books:

- God is with you, too. You may be reading about something that is close to your heart. Your emotions may be as tender as the child's as you read the story. Pray that you will have a sense of God's loving presence in your heart.

- You do not have to know the perfect answer for every question, nor do you have to answer all of the child's questions. Some of the best questions are the hardest to answer. Be sure, however, to acknowledge the child's question. Be honest. Say that you don't have the answer. If the child asks, "Why did she have to die?" it's all right to say, "I don't know."

- Pray with the child to feel God's loving presence. Let the child know that you care about him or her and about his or her feelings. Let the child know that whether he or she feels God's presence or not, God is still with him or her. This is a loving, precious, and powerful gift that you can give the child.

- Be aware that God works in a variety of ways. You may not get much of a response from the child as you read this book. Don't be concerned. Read the book at different times. You are planting a seed—a seed for the child to recognize God is at work in everyone's life.

- Have fun! Enjoy the story and this time with the child. Children are precious gifts from God created in his image. God is helping you to prepare the child for a future in his kingdom.

Dr. Scott

R. Scott Stehouwer, Ph.D., professor of psychology, Calvin College, and clinical psychologist